LOON LAKE

LOON LAKE

Ron Hirschi

Photographs by
Daniel J. Cox

COBBLEHILL BOOKS
Dutton • New York

To Shannon and all soft birds
R. H.

For my beautiful wife, Julie,
who understands the meaning
of love, patience, and hard work
D. J. C.

Library of Congress Cataloging-in-Publication Data

Hirschi, Ron.
    Loon lake / Ron Hirschi ; photographs by Daniel J. Cox.
        p.   cm.
    Summary: Text and photographs explore a northern lake and its
wildlife.
    ISBN 0-525-65046-6
    1. Lake fauna—Juvenile literature.   [1. Lake animals.]   I. Cox,
    Daniel J., 1960-   ill.
QL146.H57   1991   90-34396
591.5'26322—dc20   CIP
                            AC

Published in the United States by Cobblehill Books, an affiliate of
Dutton Children's Books, a division of Penguin Books USA Inc.

Designed by Charlotte Staub
Printed in Hong Kong   First Edition
10   9   8   7   6   5   4   3   2   1

Paddle with me
quietly, slowly.

Dragonfly

Great blue heron

Listen to the gentle lapping waves, *ga-ronck* of the great blue heron, and the soft *hummmm-buzzzzz* of dragonfly wings.

Wood frog

Watch for frogs
plopping into the
lake where the
water lilies blossom. And, listen all
the while for the song of the dancing
loons.

Redwing blackbird male

Cattails rustle near the shore. They bend beneath a redwing blackbird. The male's wings flash ruby red to attract his mate and to warn other blackbirds to stay away.

Just beyond the redwing's perch, a hungry egret stares into the shallows. Snakes, salamanders, and schools of sunfish
hide
from its
eyes.

Common egret

Muskrat hiding near opening of den

Swimming up ahead,
just beyond a painted

Trio of painted turtles

turtle sunning log, a busy muskrat
builds its waterfront lodge.

River otter

The river otter slips past too, then climbs

ashore to play on the grassy banks.

Splash! Swat! Splash! A beaver whacks the water with its tail to warn its family of danger. The beaver dives quickly. Did we paddle too close? Did the old snapping turtle frighten the beaver family?

Beaver

Beaver feeding on downed aspen tree

If we pull the canoe to the shore, maybe we can watch the beaver gnaw on willow branches or scoop mud onto its house of sticks.

Red-necked grebes at nest site

Maybe we will see a pair of red-necked grebes nesting in the reeds. And maybe, just maybe, if we watch from shore as silently as the whitetail deer, the dancing loons will come near.

Whitetail doe

Can you hear the loons singing?
Listen…Their wide wings whistle
as they fly to the lake from a distant

shore. Heavy loon bodies splash when they land—a pair looking for a safe place to build their nest.

They search for a sheltered cove or a tiny island with plenty of food nearby. If any intruders come near, they might dance their special dance. Up on their feet, the loons paddle like swimmers in a race.

Faster. Faster. Faster.
They swim side by side and
dance as only loons can dance.
    Splashing and leaping, they run
across the waves to chase other
loons that may come too near.

Adult common loon—penguin dance

The loons sing as they dance.
A-A-Whoo-Kwee-Kwee-We!
OOOO-Kweee!
Their song echoes from shore to shore.

Adult loon spreads its wings to look big and intimidating.

Leave them
now as they
swim more
quietly,
more slowly.

Adult loon dipping head into water, beginning courtship display

Leave them
now at this lake
all their own
and soon…

Loon incubating eggs

Loon turning eggs in nest

Pair of common loons with chick between them

there will be more.

AFTERWORD

We hope this introduction to loon nesting lakes will tug you down to the shore to watch for more. But, approach loon habitat slowly, carefully, quietly. Lakes can be exciting places to watch wildlife if we respect the needs of the loons, and of each of the animals living along the lakeshore.

Loons are especially sensitive to people. They need a lot of privacy. They also need clean water with lots of fish or other aquatic life. Unfortunately, many lakes have now been too thoroughly developed to support nesting loons. Others have been polluted by acid rain or other forms of contamination. Here in my home state of Washington, loons were once abundant as nesting birds. Now there are thought to be only two pairs nesting in the entire state. So, my loon watching is mainly during winter when migrating loons move down from the north to feed in the ocean or inlets of Puget Sound.

You might see loons throughout North America autumn to spring. As summer approaches, they retire to protected coves or small islands in lakes in the northernmost states and in Canada. Here they raise their young and sing their haunting, mysterious song.

The song of the loon has come to symbolize wilderness for many people. And, the struggle for survival of the loon has also come to be a special symbol for others. You can help with efforts to save loons from local extinction by joining people who work to build artificial nesting platforms, protect lakeshores from development, or attempt to keep our air and water free of pollution. Write the NORTH AMERICAN LOON FUND, RR 4 BOX 240C, Meredith, New Hampshire 03253, to learn more about loon protection efforts in your home state.